A Victim Speaks

"I'm being . . . harassed," Jerome told me. "Every day, before school. And after school. I'm getting stopped, and shaken down."

My blood was boiling already. There is nothing that enrages a superhero like the strong preying on the weak.

"What . . . is . . . his . . . name?" I asked slowly, clenching and unclenching my fists to try and channel my natural aggression. I could not let it get out of control.

Emotion is the superhero's enemy.

"Vanessa," Jerome croaked.

#4

LADIES' CHOICE

Also by Chris Lynch

•THE HE-MAN•
WOMEN HATERS CLUB
#4

LADIES'
CHOICE

Chris Lynch

📖 HarperTrophy®
A Division of HarperCollins*Publishers*

Harper Trophy® is a registered trademark of
HarperCollins Publishers Inc.

Ladies' Choice
Copyright © 1997 by Chris Lynch
All rights reserved. No part of this book may be used or reproduced in
any manner whatsoever without written permission except in the case of
brief quotations embodied in critical articles and reviews. Printed in the
United States of America. For information address HarperCollins
Children's Books, a division of HarperCollins Publishers,
10 East 53rd Street, New York, NY 10022.
Library of Congress Cataloging-in-Publication Data
Lynch, Chris.
    Ladies' choice / Chris Lynch.
       p.   cm. — (The He-Man Women Haters Club ; #4)
    Summary: The goal of the He-Man Women Haters Club, to avoid
females at all costs, is threatened when one of the members betrays the
others.
ISBN 0-06-027417-4 (lib. bdg.). — ISBN 0-06-440658-X (pbk.)
    [1. Clubs—Fiction. 2 Sex role—Fiction. 3. Humorous stories.]
I. Title. II. Series: Lynch, Chris. He-Man Women Haters Club ; #4.
PZ7.L979739Lad   1997
[Fic]—dc21   97-11651
                                                                      CIP
                                                                       AC

      1   2   3   4   5   6   7   8   9   10
                              ❖
                         First Edition
Visit us on the World Wide Web!
http://www.harperchildrens.com

Contents

1
Big Hole

They were already hating women by the time I showed up. So I didn't make the rule, I just followed it.

In those days I was a follower, not a leader.

Mothers aren't women anyway. So they are exempted. You do not have to hate your mother to be in the He-Man Women Haters Club.

You can if you want to, though. It is up to the discretion of each individual member.

I choose not to.

The woman-hating end of it is covered anyhow, by some of our other troopers. He-Man Steven, for instance. Now there's a front-line, hand-to-hand-combat-ready soldier in the girl-hating theater of operation. Especially when it comes to this person named Monica.

No, I mean *except* when it comes to this Monica person.

Wait, no. It is *especially* when it comes to Monica. At least that's how Steven tells it. It can be very difficult to tell exactly what the story is there if you just go by his actions. All I know for certain is that she must be coated in some secret sinister chemical that Steven's allergic to, because without fail every time she makes an appearance, he behaves as if he's been abducted by aliens, taken to their ship, beaten over the head with a rubber mallet, injected with central-nervous-system-disabler syrup, and then dropped back out of the ship from a height of maybe five thousand feet.

That could be hate, I suppose. So if he says he hates her, he hates her.

There is no mistaking He-Man Jerome's commitment to the cause. If Jerome was stranded at sea on a boat for a month with no food and no drinkable liquids and suddenly a delicious lobster jumped up on deck, with an unopened can of Seven-Up in one claw and a jar of cocktail sauce in the other, if that lobster happened to have long eyelashes and a ponytail, Jerome would throw himself over the side.

At first I thought it might be that Jerome—who's awfully small and a He-Man only by virtue of his membership in this club—only hated women

2

because they hated him first. But then when we became rock-and-roll superstars, Jerome was the first one to attract a groupie named Vanessa. She seemed like a perfectly normal girl to me—if such a thing exists—but Jerome reacted to Nessy as if he'd drawn the Death card from a fortuneteller.

Jerome really doesn't like 'em.

Wolfgang does, though. He-Man Wolfgang likes girls and he loves Monica and he doesn't care who knows it. So why would somebody like that be in this particular outfit? Because that's what Wolfgang's all about. That's his personality. If he hated guns, he'd join the National Rifle Association. If he hated dogs, he'd go to dog shows just to be close to everybody who completely disagreed with him. And to be the only person in the world to boo dogs.

We don't get rid of him for a couple of reasons. First, even though he's in a wheelchair, he is the toughest He-Man we've got, so not only is he very handy to have around, no one else is quite He-Man enough to tell him he's out. Second, when it came time for us to go up onstage, it was Wolf who was the front man, all fearless and hammy. Nobody else here could have done that job.

Not even the guy the band was named after. Scratch and the Sniffs's lead guitarist, Scratch, was with us for only a short while, but he made a big impact. He showed up at the same time as Cecil, a very nice fellow from Alabama who calls himself The Killer because he once killed an alligator, which actually turned out to be a big frog, which actually turned out to have been already dead when he killed it. We call him Cecil. Cecil stayed.

Scratch, though, didn't stick. He was a homeless kid, and dirty, and he'd eat anything. He sort of showed up out of no place, took us on a fun rock-and-roll ride, made everybody's life faster and louder and more exciting. He made me a star. But he didn't want to be one himself. And in the end, just before he left us, he came up big, defending the honor of the He-Men, taking on the sinister forces of sleazy adult outsiders and giving them a good whipping.

And then he vanished in the night.

We never had anyone like that here before. He was a hero, a legend. He was a real He-Man. He was an inspiration. Scratch left a big hole when he left, and only I among the He-Man Women Haters can fill a big hole like that.

Which brings me to me. My name used to be Ling-Ling.

2
A Little Problem with Reality

"You can't be serious," Jerome said grimly.

"God, I hope he is serious." Wolfgang laughed.

"Ling?" Steven asked, staring at me with a palms-up gesture of complete bafflement.

Bafflement is good. A superhero should be baffling.

"Don't call me that," I said to Steven.

"Huh?"

"Ling. Don't call me Ling. Ling is dead."

"Thank god," he responded. "Finally we get to learn what your real name is. So if Ling-Ling is dead, who's alive in there, might I ask?"

"Bolt Upright."

Steven swung around, looking away from me to address the other He-Men gathered around the 1956 Lincoln that was our headquarters. "He isn't getting any better," Steven said, exasperated. "I think his condition is deteriorating. We should call somebody."

"Don't do a thing," Wolfgang said, wheeling my way to lend me some moral support. "I think ol' Ling here—"

"Bolt," I corrected.

"Bolt. I think ol' Bolt has the right idea. I believe that what he's thinking is just the—" He interrupted himself, leaned closer to whisper to me, "What in the world *are* you thinking, anyway?"

Before I could enlighten him, He-Man Cecil came loping in. Long-striding from the front of Lars's garage to the back where we hung out, Cecil's movement spoke of hope, enthusiasm, fresh blood running through the operation, readiness to meet the challenges of the new day.

He stopped at me. He frowned his familiar dead-lost look as he took me in.

"Aw, now look at this, I'm all confused all over again," The Killer moaned. "I got to start right back at the beginning here."

It was probably my new look that had him disoriented.

Ling had been a kid. Bolt was a man, more than a man even, a superhero, but beyond a superhero. Bolt Upright was a whole different kind of being and, as such, had to look like one.

I wore a form-fitting long-sleeved black thermal

undershirt that clung to my frame like moss to a rock. I wore Lycra running shorts—black and shiny with gold lightning bolts running down the legs. I wore white golf gloves and white tennis shoes and white socks that came up over my knees because I heard a baseball player once say that if you feel fast you are fast, and that white shoes made him feel faster. He was right. I was going to be a blur. I wore one of those aerodynamic, teardrop-shaped bicycle helmets and wraparound sunglasses that made me look like a machine rather than a mere person.

It is important never to appear to be a mere person.

I wore no cape. Capes are for fools.

"I am Bolt Upright," I announced to Cecil. "I am what this organization has been sorely in need of."

"Hey," Wolf said, "why don't you call yourself Nuts instead of Bolts?"

"This is not funny," Jerome said. Jerome often says that. "He can't be out there on the street, looking like that, embarrassing the club."

"Think he'll damage our *rep*?" Wolfgang asked. Then he laughed, but I wasn't sure why. "Don't you listen to these guys, Bolt, you look just stunning. The shoes are a little bright, but . . ."

"White is the color of swiftness," I informed him.

"Ya?" Steven asked. "Well, what's the color of mental illness?"

"I can tell you are making fun of me," I informed him.

"Really?" he said.

"Yes, but I don't care. Real individuals, heroes and visionaries, they have always been mocked because they are misunderstood by the common folk. I say let 'em. Let 'em all laugh at me."

"Hey, Ling," Jerome joined in. "Check out any old movie. You know how you can tell right off which character is insane? It's always the one who says 'Let 'em all laugh at me.' And guess what? They all *do*."

Wolfgang laughed and laughed. At least one of the He-Men was having a good time.

"I get it," Cecil piped up.

Everyone turned to look. We had forgotten about Cecil.

"You get *what*?" Jerome asked.

"Bolt. Bolt Upright. I get it now. I see what he means. I see what he sees."

Jerome started waving at him. "Good-bye, Huckleberry. Have a nice voyage out there in space. Send us a postcard . . ."

"You need an assistant," Cecil said to me.

I knew this already, of course. It had kept me up all the previous night. But I never considered Cecil.

"I'll call myself The Killer," he said.

I shook my head at that. "Can't. That's your street name. You're known. Your new name has to be mysterious."

"*El Matador,*" Wolf announced loudly. "It means 'The Killer' in Spanish."

"Wow," Cecil marveled. "You do know all things. Are you a superhero too?"

"Jeez, you're a sap," Jerome barked at Cecil. "How are you going to go out there and fight evil when you can't even be trusted to cross the street by yourself?"

Jerome always took Cecil's smaller brain as an insult to his larger one.

"Maybe we won't cross streets, Jerome," I said. "Maybe we'll fly."

Jerome grabbed himself by the forehead and began massaging his temples. "This is bad. This is very bad."

"This is great," Wolf countered. "This is very very great."

Steven had jumped behind the wheel of his Lincoln, turned on the radio, and was pretending to drive really fast and far away.

Steven, I'm sorry to say, has a little problem with reality.

3
Patton and HoHos

I have to admit something. The first time I saw the movie *Patton*, I cried.

There was a time, way back when, when I used to cry a lot.

It was when he slapped the soldier. General Patton got angry, the soldier cried, Patton got angrier, slapped the kid. The kid cried some more. I joined him.

But I rented the video and forced myself to watch it again. Then I bought it, and watched it over and over and over. I love that movie now, and I especially love that scene. I look forward to it. I cheer it. When I'm in an especially good mood, I slap myself along with the movie.

So naturally as part of indoctrination, El Matador had to watch it too.

"Ouch!" he yelped when the time came for me to smack him. He rubbed his cheek and whined at me. "Whatja do that for? I didn't do nothin'. I was just sittin' here, and *bap*, you haul off and—"

Bap. I had to. He was getting hysterical.

"You do that again, and you're gonna be Bolt, but you ain't gonna be Upright no more."

"Sorry," I said calmly. "Part of the training. You and I have got to be rock hard and afraid of nothing if we want to be feared and respected throughout the neighborhood. Word has got to spread fast that Bolt Upright and El Matador are two hombres who—"

I was interrupted by a knock. "Helloo? Ling?" my mother called. We were in the cellar, where my private video and bumper-pool room was located. Mom wanted to come down from the kitchen.

"Mom, please . . ." I said as she came on down without waiting for a reply.

"*Patton*?" she asked. "Ling, you're not down here slapping yourself . . ."

"No," Cecil corrected her. "He's down here slapping me."

"I don't think that's very good either. Remember what I told you, son," she said, setting down a tray on the coffee table in front of us.

"Mother?" I asked. But it wasn't really a question as much as a request for her to go.

"Don't you 'Mother' me. You remember the

rule: If I hear any sounds of hitting behind this door—whether it's yourself you're abusing or somebody else—then you will be grounded."

"Whoa," El Matador whispered in my ear. "Would she really keep you in the house?"

"No," I said. "Just on the ground. No flying for a week."

Cecil started laughing. He stopped when he realized I had not made a joke.

"You take this superhero stuff pretty seriously, huh?" he said.

"Fighting evil is a very serious business, mister," I informed him.

"But not so serious that you can't stop for a couple of HoHos and a glass of strawberry Quik," Mrs. Ling said.

"Course not," Cecil answered, grinning broadly. "We ain't fanatics, after all."

"Yes we are," I said. "But we can still have the HoHos."

Even Patton survived having a mother, I figured.

Before long there was another interruption. The doorbell upstairs.

Mom ran to get it. We heard muffled voices, suspicious laughs. Silence.

Then, *bumpety bump de bump* down the stairs.

"I am so happy about this," Mom said. "I was so afraid that you were never going to have any friends. Now you have two."

"How did you locate my position, Wolfgang?" I asked suspiciously.

"Mat told me," he said, wheeling right past me to get to the snacks.

"Who is Mat? I don't know any Mat."

A hand slowly went up. It belonged to my associate, El Matador.

"Sorry," he said.

"We'll let it slide this time," I said. "But don't divulge our position to anyone else. Remember when Vicki Vale got into the Batcave? That was the worst poss—"

Another set of footsteps coming down the stairs.

"*There* you are," Steven said. "What, did you guys think you were starting a new club without me?"

"I'll get more HoHos," Mother said.

"An excellent idea," Wolfgang said, with a bitten HoHo already in each hand.

"Gee," I said to Steven, "why didn't you bring Jerome while you were at it?"

Steven pointed across the room, to a small rectangular window that led up to the street. There was He-Man Jerome's nervous little face.

"He didn't want to come down," Steven said. "He was afraid of your mother."

"Yes, well my mother was *supposed* to be steering people away."

"On the contrary," Wolf said. "She steered me down here. Strong woman, that mom of yours."

"Why thank you," she said, marching back in with enough snack cakes and Quik to keep the whole club satisfied for the afternoon. "There," she added, as if reading my worst fears. "Now they'll never leave."

How was I supposed to train a new man *and* defeat all the enemies of mankind if my mother wouldn't even block the door for me?

"Aw," El Matador moaned. "Look at the little feller up there. Can't we let him in?"

Jerome was busy looking like somebody's pet rabbit pressed against the glass.

"Come on down, Jerome," I called without opening the window. "My mother won't hurt you."

He shook his head silently.

"So what are you gonna do?" Wolf asked. "Just hover outside the new clubhouse every time we—"

"Hold it there, soldier. About-face," I commanded. "This is not going to be—"

I was cut off by the sad little screams outside. I

turned just in time to see Jerome airlifted from the window, his dangling arms and legs clawing and kicking at the air.

The He-Men gasped.

"What was that?" Wolfgang called.

"I never seen nothin' like that afore," cried Cecil.

"We have to save him," Steven said, rushing to the window to see.

It was as if an unseen hand, from some unknown life form, had scooped our little friend up and removed him from the surface of our humble, primitive planet.

Only I saw the hand. And the life form was not—unfortunately—unknown to me.

"So what are you doing crawling around outside my house?" asked the voice of my sister, Rock.

Steven narrated from his spot at the window. "She's got him lifted right up off the ground!"

"With one hand," I added without even looking.

"Yes. How did you know that?"

"It's my sister, home from boarding school."

"She's stronger than *you*," he said, stunned.

"She's stronger than *everybody*, *everywhere*." I sighed.

"She's carrying him now," Steven went on.

"Jerome's stopped struggling. He's hanging there in her grip like a rubber chicken."

We all sat still while we listened to my sister's size-fifteen Timberlands come pounding down the stairs. This time, of course, there was no knock at the door.

"Somebody here lose this?" Rock asked, kicking the door open. She displayed Jerome as if he was something her dog had flushed out of the bushes. "He said he was a friend of yours, Ling, but I told him that couldn't be possible since you don't *do* the friend thing."

I could have sworn her vacation wasn't until next week.

My hearty assistant, El Matador, slid behind me, shrinking from the mighty presence of Rock.

Wolf, though . . .

He wheeled right up to her, looking straight up, smiling.

"I *love* you," he said. Then he spun toward me. "I *love* her. She's so *big*. She's so *beautiful*."

Wolf was a little confused. If he was her brother, he'd be able to see her more clearly. I wanted to help him.

"She's not beautiful," I said. "She's a big fat beast."

Rock just smiled, as if she found me amusing.

"No," Wolf said, wheeling toward me. "Let me show you. *She* is a mighty sequoia. This"—I could see it coming a mile away, as he reached out both hands to grab my belly roll with both hands—"is fat."

Of course, they bonded instantly. "You know," Rock said to him, "I've tried. I've offered to train him a million times, but he refuses."

Wolf faked sincerity. "I know, I know, I've tried to train him myself. But we still have to lay newspapers all over the clubhouse floor."

So embarassing. Even Jerome was laughing, as he dangled five feet off the floor. I froze them all with a fierce glare.

Rock lowered Jerome into Wolfgang's lap, then approached me.

I braced myself for the struggle. It would not have been our first.

"Lighten *up*, will you?" she said, laughing and slipping around behind me. Then it was my turn as she hoisted me, squeezing me so tight around the waist, I could feel HoHos climbing back up my esophagus.

"Ling wants to get into the *Guinness Book*," she said to her audience, "for reaching the age of eighteen without once cracking a smile."

"You are embarassing me in front of my men."

She shook me. "Go on, have a laugh why don'tcha?"

"Laugh?" I asked over my shoulder. "At myself? I think not. I have my dignity." My shirt was rolling up over my belly and I stretched to touch the floor with my toes.

Steven walked up to us like we were a museum sculpture. "Awesome. It's a shame she's a girl."

"Shame, shmame," Wolf cracked. "We got the wrong Ling. I say we trade up and take the Rock."

4

Will the Wolf Survive?

And that's why Wolfgang, despite all his other gifts, will never rule the world. He lets his emotions get in the way of good common sense. In love? Is the boy mad?

With *my* sister?

We may have to put him down, like a broken racehorse. Because he's no good to anyone in this condition, and could very well do himself some serious harm. He wasn't a very useful He-Man Woman Hater at the moment, either.

We were back at the garage, where Steven is always at his He-Manliest.

"Hang him," Steven said calmly. "It's all you can do when a guy mutinies."

Steven was always gung-ho for punishing, expelling, or otherwise disposing of Wolfgang. They have a good inner-club rivalry going that is actually beneficial to the operation. It creates the dynamic tension that keeps us sharp. And despite what they say about each other, they have a deep mutual respect.

"Or I could shove him and his rotten smelly wheelchair off a pier into the bay," Steven volunteered.

"At ease there, soldier," I said.

"And since when are we in the army?" Jerome asked. "I thought we were more like an auto club."

"I thought we were more like the Fantastic Four," El Matador added.

"The Fantastic Four-Cylinders, how's that?" Wolfgang said, rolling into the garage to join us. "And by the way, there are five of us, piston head."

Cecil stared at the fingers of one hand, counting.

I turned on Wolf, put my fists on my hips, and stared at him through my sunglasses. I was in full Bolt Upright uniform, so I knew I had his fear and respect and attention.

"You are making a mockery of this club," I snarled.

"You know what your problem is, Ling, is that you don't look flamboyant enough. Maybe some feathers someplace might help. Some spray paint and flowers splashed about your body . . ."

"This man is not a joke," El Matador said,

rushing between us. He was wearing a cowboy hat, fake leather vest, and real spurs that jingle-jangle-jingled when he walked.

"Well then," Wolf joked, "as long as *you're* vouching for him . . ."

"I am," The Killer said.

"Can we get back to hating some women, please?" Jerome asked. "We need to get back to basics here. And I have a problem."

Now we were talking. A small, defenseless creature, needy and alone. Coming for help to Bolt Upright, the only person who could right the world's wrongs for him.

"What do you need, son?" I asked gently, yet strongly.

"Ah, you're not my father, thank you."

"That's right," Wolf said. "Pee Wee Herman's his father."

"I will quit this club right now . . ." Jerome railed on. Steven pulled an imaginary notebook out of his back pocket, made a check mark with an imaginary pencil. He does this every time Jerome quits, which means he's filled up a couple of notebooks already.

"Silence, everyone," I said, my hands straight up in the air like I was stopping traffic.

"Yes," El Matador contributed. "Silence, everyone."

"Well," Jerome started tentatively, "I'm being . . . harassed. Every day, before school. And after school. I'm getting stopped, and shaken down."

My blood was boiling already. There is nothing that enrages a superhero like the strong preying on the weak.

"What . . . is . . . his . . . name?" I asked slowly, clenching and unclenching my fists to try and channel my natural aggression. I could not let it get out of control.

Emotion is the superhero's enemy.

"Vanessa," Jerome croaked.

Steven and Wolfgang, joining forces for the first time in memory, laughed so hard the garage sounded like a packed football stadium.

"That's it!" Jerome squealed indignantly. "I'm quitting right now." He stormed off as Steven pulled out the notebook.

I pointed at Jerome, and El Matador ran to retrieve him. Jerome was kicking and clawing as he was carried back to me.

"Do not listen to them," I said. "You have nothing to be ashamed of. It doesn't matter who it is—if someone is assaulting you, and extorting money from you . . ."

"Ah . . ." Jerome said. He wasn't struggling anymore, just sort of hanging there while El

23

Matador cradled him. "She's not extorting money, exactly . . ."

"What is it then?"

"Shashkisfassisheses."

We could not quite understand him.

"What?" Wolf called. "Could you speak up there?"

Steven joined in. "Weeee cannn't heeeear youuuu."

"*Kisses!* All right? Happy now, ya savages? She's forcing me to give her a kiss or I can't cross the footbridge over the commuter rail track. . . ."

"'The Three Billy Goats Gruff'!" Steven laughed.

"So that would make you . . . don't tell me now . . . the *littlest* Billy Goat Gruff," Wolf added.

"That's it," Jerome demanded, pointing toward the exit. "Take me out of here, ya big goof."

Cecil, being a good soldier, followed orders and started carrying Jerome toward the door.

"Bring him back here," I commanded, then turned toward the troublemakers. "You two, go find something useful to do."

"Fine," Wolfgang said. "I just stopped by to say I couldn't come to today's meeting anyway. I got a date."

"Whoa," Steven said. "A *date*? Like, with a . . . grrrrrrllll?"

He sure did have trouble with that word.

"No way, junior," Wolf said, making a big show of slicking his hair back, then brushing his teeth with his finger. "I got a date with a *woman*."

"That's it!" Steven announced. "He's through. He's out. There can be no more blatant violation of our rules than coming *into* our garage, and announcing to the whole membership that he's consorting with the enemy. Taunting us with it. Let's get this over with finally. All in favor—"

"Hold on now," I said calmly. "I think we can handle this thing more smoothly, without any bloodshed. He-Man Wolfgang, with whom have you got this date?"

"You know who it is. It's the girl goddess, woman of women, the big yabba-dabba-doo herself."

"Rock."

"That's right, baby, me and the Rock."

I just had to be sure. That was a relief. I turned to Steven.

"Don't worry about it," I said. "Let him go. If my sister doesn't turn him into a lifelong woman-hater, then nothing will."

5
Bolt on the Beat

I waited.

Stealth. Was key.

I was in the bushes on one side of the bridge, while El Matador crouched in the brush on the other side. We'd left Jerome about three blocks back, with instructions to come hobbling along at precisely the time he did every morning.

Normalcy. Was another key.

"Why do we need so many keys?" Cecil asked, shattering our careful silence.

"Would you please be quiet?" I said firmly. "We are trying to be stealthy."

"You mean, like, to be good superheroes we hafta eat a lotta vegetables and get plenty of exercise, stuff like that?"

Spiderman was bitten by the radioactive spider. The guy from Kung Fu had to carry the burning pot with his bare forearms. I have Cecil.

"*Stealthy,*" I repeated patiently. "Not healthy. It means invisible, and *silent.*" I nearly yelled the word at him, which probably only confused him further.

I crossed the road to address him directly. "You are going to have to stop talking now, Cecil, or we're not going to surprise anyone." I heard myself speaking like a preschool teacher. "Now, I want you to stoop down way low in those bushes, okay? Can you do that for me?"

I watched as he bent his knees and sank.

"Shush" was the last thing I said before silently sweeping back across the road. By the time I'd resumed my hideout, Cecil had already forgotten his instructions.

"I feel like the wolf in 'Little Red Riding Hood,'" he said, giggling.

A giggling superhero. Much work to be done there.

Cecil finally stopped chatting when Jerome, as scheduled, came trembling down the road. Even though he knew perfectly well we were there, he looked like a squirrel caught on the ground a mile away from the nearest tree.

And, as promised, there was the infamous Nessy, popping up out of the shadows to intercept our boy. She looked cool and sinister, arms folded, leaning against the bridge wall. She wore a blue-and-green-plaid parochial-school uniform, and a matching headband taming her frizzy black hair.

We were not there to inflict harm on her. As I said, I do not hate women. Superheroes don't have time for that. And we didn't even intend to scare her too badly, just enough to let her know that, hey, somebody is watching, and that somebody is on the side of the weak, meek, oppressed. She'll know who we mean without our even having to mention Jerome by name.

As our little friend drew near, El Matador and Bolt Upright coiled, ready to spring. It would be quite a show, and I hoped Vanessa didn't get too terrified, but we had a job to do, and let the chips fall where they may.

Jerome began whistling bravely.

Nessy started laughing. Then, when he was within ten feet of her, she snarled, "Pucker up, ya big hunk o' man."

He told us she would say that, but it was a shock all the same. That was our cue.

I must admit, it was an awesome display. Cecil's well-worked farm-boy legs propelled him ten feet into the air as he flew toward Vanessa from one direction. He looked almost like a sky diver as he descended, hanging on to his sombrero as he parachuted to Earth. I, from the opposite side, merely charged, rhinoceroslike, right over the underbrush, the spandex of my shorts glinting in the morning sun, the whiteness of my socks, gloves, and bicycle helmet blinding to our enemies.

"Eeeeeeee!" Vanessa screamed helplessly, truly deeply pathetically scared of us.

Then we stopped before her, and stood.

We didn't, actually, have a plan beyond that point.

So we stood, dumbly.

She had a chance now to get a good look at us. We towered over her, me and Cecil, at a combined height of over twelve feet and a weight of maybe three hundred. If she stood on her toes, Nessy might have reached the minimum requirement for riding the roller coaster.

"Boo!" she screamed at us, and as the two superheroes backed up, we nearly trampled Jerome, who had been cringing around the back of our knees.

She just caught us by surprise, that's all.

We stepped right back up to her.

"Raaaaaaah!" she was roaring at us now. "What

in the heck are you two supposed to be, and what business do you have bothering us?"

"Us?" I said. "We're not bothering any 'us,' we're bothering *you*. Because you're terrorizing our weak and pathetic friend."

Jerome punched me in the back. It hurt. Guess he wasn't quite as weak and pathetic as I thought.

"Terrorizing? You two freaks need to get out and meet people a little more often. This is not terrorizing, for your information, it's *courting*. Jerome and I happen to be in love."

Jerome was now shoving both Cecil and myself from behind. "Get her," he screamed. "Jeez, would you get to work? Kill her, beat her up, maim her, or something."

"Ah, no, that's not what true superheroes do," I said, holding up one hand in the internationally recognized gesture of peace.

Apparently, Vanessa did not recognize the internationally recognized gesture of peace.

She grabbed my hand and, wrapping each of her little mitts around two of my fingers, made like a wishbone, trying to pull my hand apart at the center. "Stop picking on me," she said.

"Yeow," I yelped. "Now that is enough. I come to you in the spirit of—"

El Matador intervened, grabbing Nessy's surprisingly powerful wrist. "Don't make us get vicious, little lady."

She groaned with the effort as she kicked his ankle. (At least we were making her work to beat us up.) He released his grip on her. She kicked him again. He fell, rubbing his ankle. She kicked his hand. He was clearly beaten, down and out at this point. So she kicked him again.

"I'm talking about *love* here," Vanessa insisted. "Go on, tell them, Jerome."

"Oh my . . . oh jeez . . ." Jerome moaned, first pacing, then taking a seat on a large rock, head in hands. "She thinks we're Romeo and Juliet. I think it's more like Punch and Judy."

Quickly Vanessa turned to Jerome. She actually looked surprised. And hurt. "Oh, we need to talk," she said. "Really, Jerome, this is all happening because we are not communicating. We're going to talk a lot more from now on."

"Oh my god oh my god oh my god," Jerome said, running his hands crazily back over his head, uprooting small clumps of his own hair that then flew off in the wind.

Vanessa returned her attention to me. "But first we have to get rid of you," she said. Repeatedly and with great force, she poked her finger into my belly. "Jeepers, you're soft," she said, poking, poking again.

"All right," I said. "You've had your fun. Why don't you just—"

"What? Why don't I just leave you alone?"

"That's a thought," Cecil said from the pavement, rubbing his injured ankle.

"El Matador!" I thundered, hoping to bring him to my aid and scare Vanessa off at the same time.

Wrong and wrong again.

"Gee, I'd like to, Bolt," Cecil said, "but boy, this thing's really actin' up on me now. . . ."

Vanessa shook her head, like she was embarrassed by us. And she would not stop poking my stomach.

"Listen, you," I said. "I'm a defender of right, and a gentleman as well. I live by a strict credo that says violence is to be avoided at all costs. And my mom raised me never to strike a—"

Mommy?

As everyone knows, there is a weakness inside all superheroes, and Bolt Upright is no exception.

All of a sudden, at the mention of my mother, I was overwhelmed by a wave of sadness. I felt weak and—oh no—watery.

"Boo-hoo," Vanessa said, sticking me with that bionic finger.

"Don't. Don't say boo-hoo to me."

"Oh no!" Jerome called loudly. "Ling, not now. Not now!"

I won't. I won't. Come on, Bolt, hold it together now. You don't do that anymore. Those were the old days. You will not cry. Superheroes never, ever—

Jam. The poke. God, what does she have in that finger, a bayonet?

I couldn't even see her now, with the tears clouding my vision. It was so embarrassing. She couldn't even be bothered with me anymore. Having vanquished both Bolt Upright and the shockingly useless El Matador, Nessy went over to claim her prize. We didn't even try to stop her this time, because hey, she won him fair and square.

"*Vaya con Dios*, Jerome" was El Matador's version of helping.

Jerome was curled up in a ball on his boulder. Vanessa calmly went up to him and did the deed, right there on the lips for all the world to see. Then she gave his back a little rub and said, "See ya tomorrow," as if she was his comfort rather than his problem.

When she was safely away, I went to Jerome. He was busy rubbing his lips with his hanky. "Sure," he snarled. "You two got off easy. All *you* got was a beating." Then he leaped up and grabbed my helmet, punting it right off the bridge onto the tracks.

"You are in the wrong business," he said.

6

Bad He-Man

So maybe he did have a point. Still, I was needed. If I wasn't attempting to rescue one He-Man from the merciless, gaping jaws of love, then I was saving another He-Man from himself.

"I don't know, Steven," I said. "I'm not completely comfortable with the idea. It sounds a lot like spying."

He-Man Steven and I were deep into a stage-three, super-secret conference. That's the highest level of confidential we have so far. Stage one is low-level club secrecy, which basically means we kick Steven's uncle Lars out of the area for our meeting. Stage-one topics would include, oh, what we wanted to get for lunch, or whether any member has got the same underwear on from the previous day. Mostly stage-one secrecy is an excuse for booting Lars. When we get to stage two, we again get to eject Lars, but also we move the conference into Steven's 1956 Lincoln just in case any foreign agents are around trying to pull any He-Man Women Hater information for their evil use. Again, stage two is not usually earthshaking secrecy as much as it is a reason for us to close ranks. Sometimes we even nap in the car during stage two.

But stage-three conferences are a different matter entirely. They are rarely called and usually cause trouble, since they involve the exclusion of some or all of the other club members. On this day Steven requested a one-on-one stage three on the grounds of serious security threats within the operation. So how could I say no?

And—unprecedented in the entire history of the club—Steven allowed somebody other than himself to be the driver of his car. This had to be very important to him.

"You make it sound dirty," he pressed on. "It's not spying, it's a strategic clandestine operation."

I did like the sound of that. I beeped the horn.

"Well, that does sound a little better. But still, there has to be sufficient justification for me to approve such a thing."

"Sufficient? Sufficient? What kind of leader are you? We have the greatest justification there is: You are about to lose one of your men to the enemy. Would a really great leader allow that to happen? I think not."

He was right, of course. If a leader was any kind of decent chief at all, then that had to be the bottom line: The loss of one of your men was unacceptable. But where Steven and I weren't quite on the same page had to do with identifying the enemy. I wasn't exactly sure who the enemy was. He had no such problem.

"She's a *grrrrrlllll*, for cryin' out loud, man. How can you let her get her hands on poor old Wolfgang? He is your responsibility, you know. Our mission here is clear to me, and if it's not to you, I'll spell it out: We will rescue our brother Wolfgang from the hands of any and all women, whether he likes it or not, no matter what it takes."

Steven must have raised his voice just a bit too high, because shortly after the mention of He-Man Wolf's name, said member happened to casually wheel himself right up to the driver's side window of the car. He began wiping the glass without being asked to, like one of those dirty guys at stoplights with a squirt bottle and a squeegee. I pounded on the glass and chased him away.

"So since when are you all concerned about

what happens to him?" I asked. Wolf had wheeled around to Steven's window. Steven pounded the glass.

"Hey," Steven said, putting his hand on his chest like he was going to take the Pledge of Allegiance. "Wolfgang is very important to me. I mean, we may have our differences from time to time, but he's a member of the brotherhood, after all, and that's what counts. Am I right?"

"Okay, seems like we're honor bound. So then what is it we have to do?"

"Now you're talkin'," he said, clapping his hands and rubbing them together anxiously. "First thing is, move over—I'm drivin'."

There are three ways in and out of my rec room. One way is to go up the stairs into the kitchen. The second is through the bulkhead to freedom. The third leads into the utility room/noxious chemical repository where my mom stores the paints, solvents, and adhesive substances she uses to deface our home. The first is used by everybody. The second only by meter readers and certain wheelchair-bound He-Man visitors. The third by nobody in his right mind.

The day of Operation Save the Wolf came only

two days after Operation Save Jerome, so I figured I'd better get it right this time or face Operation Lose the Ling. He-Men Bolt and Steven were sitting for an hour and a half among the oily rags, petrified paint brushes, and caulking guns of the utility room, peering through cracks in the tongue-and-groove pine panelling that separated the basement cells. Waiting for the objects of our surveillance.

"Do you have a headache?" I asked Steven.

"Maybe I do," he answered defensively. "But that's a small price to pay for the cause."

"What about dizziness? Blurred vision?"

"No," he snapped, his face glued to the wall.

"Look at me," I said.

"I'm busy."

"There's nobody in there. You've been staring at my mother's Eisenhower painting for an hour. Ike's not going anyplace, Steven. Now turn this way."

He did, facing me full-on.

"See," he said. "Steady as a rock."

"Ya," I said. "Exactly. You are about as steady as the Rock. And if you think *I'm* bad, wait till you meet her up close and personal. She's *long* gone. You should see the stuff she does."

"Like what?"

"I'll tell you like what. Like, okay, she runs. She leaves the house and runs, sometimes for miles, for no reason. Nobody's chasing her or anything, she just runs, because she *likes* it. How's that for nuts?"

He paused. He stared at *me*, like there was something wrong with *me*.

"All right," I went on. "Also, sometimes she walks up hills, and mountains even, just for fun. She even belongs to a group where they all do it. How 'bout that? Sure wouldn't want to meet up with that bunch of loonies in a dark alley, huh?"

Still, he stared. "You're not exactly a fitness nut, are you, Ling?"

"I'm not a nut of any kind!" I insisted, though I didn't mean for it to come out so strong. "Anyway, the point is she'll probably kill us if she catches us here. Unless we're already dead from the vapors by the time they find us."

I was about to leave when we heard the slam of the bulkhead door being dropped against the side of the house. The two of us scrambled to the crack to watch.

"Careful, honey," came Wolfgang's voice from outside. Rock was dragging his wheelchair down the steps for him. "That's a precision piece of equipment there—just like myself."

"Oh please," she said, and dropped the chair down hard.

"No, really. I won the Boston Marathon three times in that chair. This year I was so far ahead, I rolled the last six miles backward. They asked me not to come back anymore because I'm demoralizing all the other crips."

Rock just laughed as she carried Wolf down the stairs and placed him gently in his seat.

"How romantic, you carrying me over the threshhold," Wolf said.

Steven pulled away from the crack and closed his eyes tight. "Ling, I'm gonna barf. If this is where he's starting from, where is it going to lead? I don't think I can take it."

"I tried to tell you," I said. "A person's got to have an awfully strong constitution for this kind of surveillance work. This is the way the pros always uncover the most disgraceful, stomach-turning stuff about a guy."

"Wanna stick pins in my toes?" Wolf offered Rock.

"See what I mean?" I shrugged. "You never know what a guy will say or do when he doesn't know you're watching." Steven gagged.

"Get away from me, you," Rock said to Wolf.

41

But she was still laughing.

"No kidding, you'll love it. I don't flinch at all. It's just like sticking a potato."

"Well, that's a refreshing change. With most of the guys I've dated, it was the head that was the potato part."

"Most?" It was my turn to be disgusted. "Who's she kidding with that 'most' business? How do you figure what's 'most' of two? She's dated two guys her whole life, and one of them hardly counts since he was our mailman and the federal government *forced* him to come to the house every day. She met him at the door once in a bathing suit and he maced her."

Steven was having an unusually confused day. "I can't tell with you, Ling—since you never joke or laugh or smile—when you're exaggerating, or just plain making stuff up."

I pointed at myself to help him along. "I tell *all* the truth, *all* the time, mister."

He pointed at me too. "Did you take *all* your medication today, *all* in one gulp?"

There's nothing you can do with him when he's like that.

Wolf pulled us back into the action. "You poor thing," he consoled the big brute. "It's lucky for you that I came along to restore your faith in guys."

"Can we take an emergency vote to stomp him to death?" Steven asked quite seriously.

"Shhh," I said, listening with fascination now.

"Speaking of guys," my sister asked mischievously, "what about *your* guys? The He-Boys. The Womanators or whatever it is my brother and his pukey little friends call themselves. Is this allowed, this fraternizing you're doing?"

"Them guys." Wolfgang laughed. "They don't tell me what to do. I just joined their jerky little club for a laugh. And because they begged me. As a matter of fact, they pay *me* dues to keep coming. And even if they did try and stop me from seeing you, they know they'd be in deep sneakers then. Why, the toughest guy they've got—after me of course—is probably Steven . . ."

Steven visibly relaxed, hearing this, nodding approval.

". . . and I've slapped *his* stupid fanny around the block so many times already, the neighbors must think I'm his dad."

Steven gritted his teeth. "I'm gonna killll you, *Dad*," he growled.

"Did you hear something?" Rock asked Wolf.

I slapped Steven on the arm to shut him up.

"Nah," Wolf said, while staring directly at us.

"Think he heard?" I asked.

"I hope so," Steven answered. "I want him to come in here so I can stick his little bat face into a can of Dutch Boy sunflower yellow and hold it there until—"

I shushed him again so we could listen to find out what Wolf knew.

"Anyway," Wolfgang went on, "you're way more He-Man than any of those guys, if you don't mind my sayin' so."

"Certainly not," my lovely sister crowed, puffing up her already well-puffed self.

"Look at these muscles of yours," he said, and wheeled himself right up to her to give her biceps a squeeze.

"*That*'s it," Steven announced. "That's all she wrote. Physical contact right before our eyes. You know the bylaws, Ling, just as well as I do. He's *outta* here." Steven turned from me to Wolf, through the crack. "You're *outta* here," he repeated. "Pack your stuff and clear out."

I actually had to grab the back of Steven's shirt and yank him down onto a five-gallon tub of spackle. He'd been waiting for this moment for quite some time, and could not control himself now that it had arrived. There were little foamy bits of spittle at the corners of his mouth. "Now you sit there," I said, "or you're going to blow our cover."

He stood up. I shoved him back down. "That's insubordination, mister," I warned him. "If you don't watch it, you'll find yourself on trial right alongside him."

Steven's eyes brightened. "There's going to be a trial? Really? You're not just saying that to make me happy?"

"No. There is going to be a trial. Now sit there and be quiet while I gather evidence."

Steven sat, and even folded his hands. But he couldn't help bouncing up and down like a little kid waiting for the show to begin.

I went back to the crack. Rock was flexing everything she had for Wolf's approval. "That's another thing," I said. "She even enters contests, with a bunch of other nuts just like her doing this. . . ." I broke into a spontaneous imitation of her posing, flexing, hulking routine.

Steven laughed at me. "See, you can be funny when you try."

I was not trying. I went back to eavesdropping.

"Where'd you get all that physique?" Wolf asked.

"I'm an athlete," she answered casually. "I work out. And I throw the javelin at my boarding school."

And I bet they throw it back, I wanted to say. But she does throw the javelin. She's not on any teams, mind you, she just throws it. The big Amazon savage.

"Wow," Wolfgang said to her, clapping. "You're almost a *guy*."

"Thanks," she said. "So are you."

Wolf laughed hard at that. "Good one there, Miss Rock. Mind if I use that line on your brother?"

"You can try. But I warn you, he doesn't understand jokes."

Sure I do. Ever heard the one about the He-Man who got himself court-martialed?

7
Wolf's Way

Steven came in with Jerome as I sat contemplating what General Patton would do if he was me. Jerome was trembling, whimpering, and clutching an envelope in his little porcelain fist. Steven was whistling a happy tune, with a new spring in his step.

"Is he here yet?" Steven asked anxiously. "Can we start the festivities? Come on, come on, let's get crackin'."

"Steven," I said, walking up to the obviously stricken Jerome, "can't you see that your friend is in distress here? Don't you care?"

He took a quick glance over at Jerome, who was shaking so hard his pants were sliding right off him.

"Ya, I see," Steven said. "But he's always nervous about something. He'll feel better after we dump Wolfgang. You'll feel better too. Everybody will feel better. Isn't it a beautiful day outside?"

Jerome stopped his nervous breakdown long enough to get a load of little Stevie Sunshine. "Does this club have a drug-testing policy?" he asked.

Steven laughed. "Good one, Jerome."

I reached out and pried the envelope out of Jerome's death grip. "Is this it?" I asked. "Is this what's bothering you?"

He nodded.

"Can I read it, then?"

He nodded.

I opened it up, unfolded the sheet of yellow lined paper, and looked at the message, printed in a variety of typefaces and styles and sizes cut from magazines and newspapers. Your basic maniac note. It read: *Dear Boyfriend . . . uh-oh . . . I love you. I know you love me too. It's cute that you're shy. But you can stop it now. We will be together for eternity.*

Also, my birthday is coming up, on the seventeenth. Make it something special, darling.

"She is a very confused girl," I said calmly. "But I don't think you should worry too much about it."

"Don't worry too much?"

"Right," I said. "Clearly, she thinks a great deal of you. She even uses the word 'love' in there somewhere."

"Love!" Jerome screamed at me. "This girl can't tell the difference between love and manslaughter. Look at this," he said, seizing the letter. "Look here. It says 'eternity.' You know what that means?"

"Ah, I think so," I said.

"It means death," he said hysterically. "She is talking about my death!"

He is a very excitable boy. You had to read pretty hard, I thought, to find death in there.

He threw the letter on the ground and made a wild dash for the Lincoln. He launched himself into the backseat and slammed the door. Steven, Cecil, and I followed. Steven opened the front door and took up his usual spot as driver. Cecil took shotgun, and I sat with Jerome, to lend him my wisdom and comforting presence.

Jerome sat hunched over, hyperventilating, with his head between his knees. "*What* am I going to get her for her birthday?"

Cecil tried to help. "Chocolates, or a nice hat . . ."

I put a finger to my lips to quiet Cecil.

Steven was still having fun. "It's your own fault, Jerome, ya stud monkey. Turn off the old magnetism once in a while, give everyone a rest."

Jerome buried his face again, moaning.

"You're not really helping things," I said to Steven. Then, back to Jerome. "Don't you worry, son, I'll fix this for you."

His head popped up, his eyes spinning madly as he stared into me. "Oh, a *fat* lot of help you'll be," he snapped.

Ouch. Jerome could be a vicious little terrier sometimes.

"You tried once already, and you made it worse, remember?" he added.

That one little failure was going to haunt me until we freed Jerome from his Vanessa problem.

Even though it was the quietest sound in the now-buzzing clubhouse, Wolfgang's confident little laugh cut right through all the clatter, and everybody looked.

He was leaning in through Cecil's window, Jerome's fan letter in his hand.

"This is sweet," he said.

"It's not sweet," Jerome responded. "It's a death threat."

"No it isn't. I know Vanessa. She just gets a little overzealous sometimes. It's her way of expressing affection, that's all."

"Well I don't want *any* affection," Jerome snapped.

Wolf chuckled, but he was laughing alone now. Even Steven's high spirits dropped when Wolfgang showed up.

"You want me to take care of this for you, little man?" he asked.

Jerome stood up—he could actually stand up inside the car. "Can you, Wolf? Can you? Would you?"

"Can I? Come on now, you know better than to ask me a dumb question like that. And would I? Of course I would. I'd do anything for one of my brothers. This is a brotherhood, ain't it?"

Wolfgang stared straight at He-Man Steven when he said it. It was pretty hard to miss the irony of all this. The "brotherhood" had two basic problems going at the moment, and Wolfgang was making himself front-and-center a part of both: He-Man Jerome had a girlfriend he didn't want to have; and He-Man Wolfgang had a girlfriend none of the other He-Men wanted him to have.

Steven, in turn, looked straight at me. "Just hold it right there," Steven said. "He's not doing any more—"

"No," I said, cutting him off. "If He-Man Wolf can fix He-Man Jerome's problem, then that's the right thing to do."

"Oh thank you, thank you, thank you," Jerome said, leaning over and shaking Wolfgang's hand a hundred times. "You're the best. You're the He-Mannest. You want money? I think I can scare up . . ."

"No thanks necessary," Wolf said with a wink. "You know me. Just doing my part for the cause, gentlemen."

Again he stared right at Steven as he said it, smiling as he backed away from the car and wheeled himself out to track down the dreaded Nessy.

"I knew it," Steven said as soon as Wolfgang was gone. "He knew we were there watching him the whole time. The rat. You're not going to let him get away with this are you, Ling? Ling? Are you?"

This was a dilemma.

"Wait," Jerome said. "Get away with what? He knew you were where the whole time?"

"We spied on the rat, that's what," Steven blurted. "He was found to be with a girl, con-sorting, even touching her muscles, and even slan-dering other He-Man members." Steven puffed way up, his eyes bugging out, his fists punching his own thighs as he talked. "So, He-Men, what do you think of *that*?"

There was a pause. Cecil broke it.

"Why'd y'all have to go spyin' on the boy to find that out? He does all that right here in front of our faces."

Jerome looked at Steven with a deep frown. "Spying's pretty low there, Steve-o."

Steven huffed, scrambled out of the car, and lay down face-up on the creeper. Then he wheeled himself under the front end to pretend to be fixing it.

"So," Cecil asked, "you gonna be kickin' ol' Wolf out of the club?"

I sighed. The pressure, the strain of command decision-making. Wolfgang was a problem, no doubt about it, a wild card. But at the same time he was probably the He-Man with the greatest ability to go out and make things happen. He was our can-do guy.

Unfortunately, some of the things he can-do you wish he wouldn't-do.

"There is an investigation under way. I cannot comment on an ongoing investigation."

I have all the CNN Pentagon press briefings on tape.

Jerome turned to me and began poking me in the belly just like Vanessa had. Very embarrassing.

"If you dare get in Wolf's way before he completes his mission, I'll bop your brains out," he warned.

It had come to this: Jerome was threatening to beat me up.

8

The Solution

Wholesale changes were in order.

The first step was going to be the most painful, but I was certain it had to be taken.

Bolt Upright must die. No one respected him, no one understood him, and anyway I was always more of a military man than a do-it-yourself superhero anyway.

So I returned the bicycle helmet and shorts to my sister. ("So *that's* where my stuff's been disappearing to," she growled. "I just TKO'd the dog when it should have been you, ya pervert.") I returned the white knee socks and Rockport striders to my mother. ("Ling, you scamp. I almost had to quit my Tuesday mall-walking club. I'm also missing a lipstick and an eye pencil—would you have any idea . . .") And I marched—literally—down to my friendly neighborhood Army-Navy Store. Time to get serious.

By the time I'd returned to the garage, I had it. Tasteful. I looked at my reflection in the door of the black Lincoln. (Steven never stopped polishing the thing.) Tasteful and dignified. You just had to respect the man in this uniform.

It was all army—the grunt branch of the service. Shiny black boots, dark-green pressed khakis, and matching blazer with a very modest set of bars on each shoulder. The hat too was dark green, flat, and crisp, with a brilliantly shiny black brim. The one shot of flash I allowed myself: a riding crop. I couldn't exactly quit cold turkey after all.

I saluted myself in the car door.

"Are we off on a mission, Bolt?" Cecil asked, coming up from behind and shocking me.

"Don't ever sneak up on a trained fighting man like that," I barked. "You want to get yourself killed?"

"Um, well no, Bolt, I sure don't."

"Don't call me Bolt." There was a small catch in my throat here. "Bolt is no more. And take off that ridiculous cowboy outfit. You look like a fool."

Cecil took off the hat and sat right down on the garage floor in a confused heap. He unstrapped his spurs.

"Where's Wolfgang?" Jerome asked, buzzing around the garage like a bumblebee. He zipped over to the car, looked inside, looked underneath. "Where is he? He was supposed to have straightened out Vanessa by now."

"At ease, soldier," I called.

"Shut up, Captain Crunch," he responded.

See what I mean. This was very very bad.

"He ain't here yet, Jerome," said Cecil. "Sit down and relax, will ya boy? You're making me nervous."

Jerome did sit right down on the floor next to Cecil, but somehow he managed to seem as if he was still running.

"Well . . . anyway . . . I just need to know . . . you know . . . if he took care of it . . . you know . . . my little problem . . . you know, like he said. He does always do what he says he's going to do, doesn't he?" Jerome hopped back to his feet and started pacing.

I got my slapping hand limbered up.

"All right, where is the four-wheeled rat?" Steven snarled as he came in. "I want to see some results. Is little Jerome a free man, or does he get to live out the rest of his days pinned like a beetle bug to the wall of Nessy's cave?"

"Oh my god oh my god oh my god," Jerome said.

I was getting very agitated about now.

"Hasn't anybody even noticed my new outfit?" I asked.

"Somebody's got to do something. Wolf's not coming," Jerome wailed. "He's never coming back. They're going to mail him back to us in pieces like the Mafia does, I just know it. Hide me, somebody hide me . . ."

I slowly approached Jerome, my riding-crop hand raised and ready to calm him down.

"Ohhhh no you don't," he said. "You just go right ahead and start slapping yourself. I'm not hysterical. You saw her. You know. I'd be insane if I *wasn't* in a panic."

He was certainly convincing. I paused to think about it, standing there with my sharp-pressed uniform on and my hand way up in the air.

"Still, it could only help you," I said, and ran after him.

I suppose some might have thought it a little bit funny, the way I had to chase Jerome around and around the car, me being so much bigger than him, and him being so wiry and crazy with fear. But I was willing to risk some ridicule to get this operation back in working order.

"Slow down so I can slap you," I said, reasonable as you please.

"Oh right," he answered. "Now who's the mental case?"

"Would you just let me slap you and get it over with, and we'll all feel better?" I said, getting increasingly wheezy and angry with the pursuit.

That was when gallant Cecil intervened. He stepped in front of me, locked a good solid grip on my upper arms, and fixed his eyes on mine.

"General," he said evenly, "I think maybe this is not exactly the leadership style you had in mind."

Gasping, gasping, I looked at Cecil, then across the roof of the car at Jerome, who was over there on his side panting, panting, his tongue visible like a little dog in summer heat.

"Here, Jerome," Steven said, walking over and taking him by the hand. "Let me show you what I do to decompress in times of great stress." And he led Jerome over to the four-wheeled creeper that lay behind the tail of the car. Steven guided Jerome down onto it, laying him flat on his back so that he was staring up at the ceiling. "Now," Steven said, "what you do is, you push off with your feet like so, sort of walking yourself under the car. Then once you are under there, you look up into the soul of the machine, at the pipes and plugs, bushings and springs and hoses, and you just contemplate it. You know what that means, J, to contemplate it?"

Jerome, remember, has about three spare IQ

points for every hardworking one of Steven's.

"Yes, I think I do," Jerome hissed.

"Good. What I think is, what I get out of this is what some geeks get out of staring up into the solar system with a telescope. This here is the whole Man's universe, all you'll ever need, right up under here. So go on now, push yourself off. And while you're there, trying to figure stuff out, if you feel like working on something, go right ahead, kid. I'll fix it later. The important thing is, just lie under there and cooooool out. You'll see, it works."

Jerome nodded silently, with a determined look on his face. He planted his feet and pushed off.

As hard as he possibly could. He was torqued up like a mainspring, because when he shoved off, he shot himself under the car, along the whole length of it, popped out the front end, and hummed right along until he crashed, headfirst, into a stack of empty motor-oil cases that came tumbling down on top of him in a heap.

"How come nobody told me we had Jerome-bowling scheduled for today?" Wolfgang said as he reappeared. "I would have worn my glove."

Wolf was clearly the man of the hour, and every-body wanted to get at him. First one to reach him—despite the new egg on his forehead, and

having to wrestle his way out of a stack of oily car-
tons—was Jerome. "So what did you do? What did
she say? What did you say? Is she dead? Did you
bring us her heart or her broom or something so I
can be sure it's safe to go outside again?"

Wolfgang reached out and patted Jerome on his
cheek.

"Don't pat me, Wolfgang," Jerome said. "Talk
to me."

Wolf answered him very confidently, very charm-
ingly. "Not to worry, not to worry, brother He-Man.
Contacts have been made. Processes have been
initiated. A positive outcome is assured."

Jerome spun around to look at me. "What is he
saying, huh? Can you tell me what he's saying?
Does anybody know what he is saying?"

"Ya," Steven said, in that tone he uses when he's
challenging Wolf. It sounds like the low gurgly-
growl dogs use when they're circling each other.
Steven went right up close to Wolfgang and
smirked at him. "I know what it means. It means
he didn't do nothing. It means he's been pulling
everybody's chain around here, like usual."

"No. As a matter of fact, it means I have been
very busy with this," said Wolf. "I have made contact with Vanessa, but since my reputation is *so*

huge, and I am so intimidating, she has refused to meet me face-to-face alone. Fortunately, our mutual friend Rock has agreed to act as mediator, and I just wanted you all to know that I am on my way over to Rock's house right this—"

"Oh *that* does it," Steven thundered. "This guy is such a crock. He ain't doin' nothing but going off on another date. He couldn't get anywhere with Vanessa, and he's not even man enough to admit it, so he's just running away to join the enemy."

Wolfgang brought his hand up to where his heart was supposed to be. "Steven," he said in a wispy voice, "I am hurt. To think that you would believe . . ."

"Save it, slick. Ling," Steven said, "I say we don't let this guy go *anywhere* without us." He turned to Wolf. "We're goin' with ya. Hah!"

"Oh no," Wolfgang protested, weakly. "No, you can't . . ."

"Oh no," Jerome protested, a lot more convincingly.

"Oh yes," Steven said. "Your game is up. Wherever you go, we go. And if Vanessa doesn't show up at Ling's house, you're history."

A loud, nervous gulp echoed through the garage.

It was Jerome, of course.

9

Apocalypso

We went through with it, though none of us expected Vanessa to be there. But that didn't stop Jerome from singing his "oh my god" song softly all the way.

And it didn't stop the clever Wolfgang from constantly assuring us that she would be there.

"Really, guys," Wolf said one last time as we circled around to the back of my house. "She's here, so why don't you all just go back—"

"I can't wait," Steven said, slapping his hands together.

The bulkhead to the cellar flew open and up out of the grave came my great big ghoulish sister Rock.

"They wouldn't believe me, honey," Wolfgang explained as she lifted him out of his chair and cradled him in her arms. "I feel so hurt. Can somebody please meet me at the bottom of the stairs with my wheels? You there." He gestured toward

Steven. "Be a good boy, would you?"

Steven was by now putting on quite a show with the number of colors he could make his face turn.

"You guys are so suspicious all the time," Rock said, shaking her head. "Don't you ever take a break from being paranoid?"

"No," I snapped.

When we got to the foot of the stairs, there she was, Vanessa, sitting on the couch, hands folded, staring at us.

I was surprised—and relieved. I was hoping we would be able to rehabilitate He-Man Wolf, and this was a good sign.

Steven was not quite so impressed. "So he got lucky. Vanessa happened to be here, coincidentally. Let's just get this over with."

"All right," Wolf said, rubbing his hands together as if he was sitting down to a nice meal. "I believe I have come up with an idea that will help not only Jerome but every He-Man with his girl problem. I am certain, in fact, that by the time we leave this room, we will all be better men, and you will all be thanking your ol' buddy Wolfgang for helping out."

As if on cue (had Wolfgang even rehearsed his speech?) my sister walked to the steps leading up to the main part of the house. She stopped at the light switch. Slowly, she turned the dimmer down, down.

"Hey," I called. "I don't like this. Rock. Rock, you put those lights back up now." She did nothing. "I mean it." Nothing. "I mean it now. Don't make me come up there now . . ."

She giggled and turned the lights down to where we could barely see each other. "Roooooock," I moaned, "you're embarrassing me again in front of my men." I stomped one big boot and slapped my leg with my riding crop.

A body moved in the darkness, brushed by me like the first pass of the shark in *Jaws*.

"Uh-oh." Suddenly it occurred to me that Jerome had not whimpered in some time. I felt around for him, pulled him close enough for me to see his face. His mouth was wide open in a futile attempt to scream.

Steven got panicky. "What's going on here? Wolf? Wolfgang, what is going on here?"

When Wolf didn't respond, I knew we had big problems.

"Retreat, men!" I called. "It's a setup! Retreat!"

We ran, as a fumbling group, toward the bulk-head.

Slam! Someone had that closed, and locked.

"This way!" I said, leading Steven, Jerome, and Cecil back toward the upstairs. There was an awful lot of giggling going on. Much more than from the two girls plus my mother we saw in the light.

Something was very wrong.

When I reached the stairs, a familiar hard finger jabbed my belly. "Get out of love's way," Vanessa told me.

"Turn around," I yelled at all the He-Men banking up against my backside. "Out through the utility room! Steven, you remember."

"Ya," Wolf called. "Steven, you remember the utility closet, ya sneaky spy."

The giggling got louder and seemed to come from the walls.

Then there was music.

Caribbean music. Loud, with a powerful beat.

"Hurry, hurry hurry," I said. "This is what they did in *Apocalypse Now*, blasting music before they wiped everybody out."

It was "Under the Sea," from *The Little Mermaid*.

By the time Steven grabbed the door handle to the utility room, the music had been turned up loud enough to shake the Eisenhower picture down off the wall with a crash.

It was just like in the war movies. Steven, poor son of a gun, never got to turn that door handle. They turned it for him.

Ahhhhhh! They poured out of that closet like wasps out of a nest, squealing, bouncing, jumping as the lights came halfway back up again. Girls. Hundreds of them, millions of them, an endless army of them, many in that familiar uniform of the Girl Scout brigade, moving to the music and over-running us.

It was uncanny the way they could synchronize their body movements precisely to the music. It must be a girl skill.

"Holy—" Steven screamed, his last words before the final, utter collapse of our line. Their laughing leader advanced on him, her hands extended toward him. He wailed, "Head for the hills, boys, it's a *dance parrtyyyy*. . . ."

Words can scarcely describe the horrors that ensued. They were a brilliant, merciless force. They divided us in the dark and never let us recombine to defend ourselves. After "Under the Sea" came the slow song "Kiss the Girl." (Monsters! Is there no end to the carnage?) By the time the lights came back up, Nessy was holding

Jerome as if he was an air mattress she was trying to expel all the air from. Sure, his feet were moving, and he appeared to be responding to the music, but that was just some residual nerve twitching like when you pinch the head off a bug. Really, he was gone, his head lying back on his neck like it was going to fall off.

I begged my mother to put a stop to it. How could she have allowed my sister to con her into this whole fiasco?

"I've been waiting for this, Ling, to see girls here. I wondered if it would happen for you someday. Your father said we would never live to see it, god rest his soul."

What *had* my rotten sister been telling her?

Cecil, our shell-shocked soldier, had cornered himself, down on his haunches in the most inaccessible crevice in the room, with his two great bony hands extended in karate-chop position. He remained frozen there like an indoor gargoyle until the doors finally opened and he flew.

But our wounds were mostly superficial compared to what happened to Steven. Monica pursued him, first to one corner of the room, then the next, then the next. Like an expert boxer, she cut off the ring, making his maneuvering room smaller and smaller, until she had him trapped. At that point things got so intense, Steven's face became a thing I did not even recognize as him. Words were exchanged over the relentless, remorseless music. She bore down on him, pressuring, leaning, until, somehow, she broke him. Broke his mind, broke his spirit.

Numbly, he followed her. Through the crowd, and into the utility closet, where she closed the door behind them. She held him trapped in there for a good seven minutes anyway.

God only knows what happened to him. Like all traumatized victims of war, he couldn't even speak of it afterward.

Fortunately I escaped harm. No one asked me to dance.

Wolfgang watched his malicious handiwork with a frightening grin. He lapped it all up the same way he lapped up the salsa, sticking his fingers into the bowl, licking them, then sticking them right back into the bowl again.

This time his violations could not be overlooked.

10
The Setup

Jury selection, of course, was the first hassle. I thought it made sense to have a small, intimate military-style tribunal made up of just official He-Men. You know, to keep it in the family. The accused, however, had other ideas.

"First," said Wolfgang, "the law says that I am entitled to a trial before a jury of my *peers*. And since the dictionary describes a peer as one's equal, I think we can agree that I don't have any of those here in the house."

"Well . . ." I said. He had me back on my heels, as usual. We were involved in a stage-three secrecy meeting inside the Lincoln, a man-to-man pretrial hearing.

"Second, if you are going to call all your jurors as witnesses, then that would seem to stack the deck against me right from the start, and that's no good either."

"Yes, but—"

"So, what I was thinking was . . ."

It was as if it was *my* pretrial hearing. As in most situations, Wolfgang was cool and in control, totally relaxed in the face of his impending public disgrace.

"Why don't you just run your own trial then, Wolfgang?" I huffed when he let me into the conversation.

"Well, if you want it run *right*, then I probably should."

I turned away from him to look to my men, who were gathered in a quivering pack outside the passenger-side window.

Yes, Wolfgang had even snagged the driver's seat.

He tooted the horn. "The only fair thing is that you go right ahead and call your witnesses, but I— since I will be acting as my own lawyer . . ."

Gulp!

". . . will call my own defense witnesses."

Not only was Wolfgang being extremely helpful in his own prosecution—he was treating it more like a party in his honor—he was looking forward to it.

"So," he said, clapping his hands. "When can we get started? I've got invitations to send out, you know, a caterer to hire . . ."

See?

"Wait here," I said as I threw open my door.

"I'll try to keep myself amused."

The three of them inched closer as I got out and slammed the door behind me.

"So what did he say?" Jerome asked. "Did he squirm? Does he want to plea bargain?"

"Well . . . it's kind of tough to tell with him . . . you know, with his legs not working and all . . . but ya, I think I saw him sort of squirm once there. . . ."

"I never been so a-scared in my whole life," Cecil said, staring off past me. This was not news. This was basically the only sentence Cecil had spoken since the Massacre at Casa Ling.

Steven didn't say anything right off, just listened attentively. Curiously Steven, who had really been the driver of the bus in the move to oust Wolfgang, had fallen largely silent in the days following the incident.

The poor, shattered He-Man.

On the other hand Jerome was invigorated. Motivated. Rabid.

"So what do we get to do to him after we find him guilty? Can we go over the punishment options once more?"

"Slow down, slow down," I said.

The Lincoln's horn beeped. Two long toots, then a short one.

"Hey," came Wolf's muffled voice as he tapped himself on the wrist where his watch would be if he owned one. "Step it up; I got a date."

"Ya, *you* got a date all right," Jerome yelled, leaning and pointing in Wolf's direction. "You got a date with *jail*," he said, a little dramatically.

I actually had to pull him back. "Ah, Jerome, I don't quite think we have the jurisdiction . . ."

Steven spoke cautiously. "Anyway, what's he saying in there? Does it look like he's gonna, you know, go quietly?"

I tried to screw up my most quizzical-looking face for him. "Are you kidding? Wolfgang? I think he's going to call the newspapers to cover the trial."

"Oh," Steven said thoughtfully. "That isn't good."

"So what?" Jerome yapped. "Let him call the newspapers and Court TV and Oprah Winfrey if he wants. We'll show the world what a rat he is."

"I never been so a-scared in my whole life," contributed Cecil.

Jerome was so blinded by rage, he could not look ahead to how this might not turn out to be so much fun after all. And Cecil, he couldn't see a hand in front of his face. Only Steven and I were starting to get the picture. Not a pretty picture.

"You know," I said, "I just don't think it's fair to put poor Cecil through a trial, to force him to relive it all . . ."

"Ya," Steven rushed in. "To have him up there on the stand recounting the whole mess . . . that would be cruel. I suggest we offer Wolfgang a dishonorable discharge, tell him to get his Woman-loving butt out of our club and never come back."

"Good plan, He-Man," I said, and offered him a salute from my sweaty brow. He saluted back, and everything was looking fine.

"You two make me *sick*," spat Jerome. "After what he did to us? After the torture . . . now you want to back down and let the snake just slither out of town? Dishonorable discharge? I'll give him a dishonorable discharge off the tip of my work boot."

Wow. Jerome was off. I didn't even dare point out to him that he was wearing cream-colored canvas boat shoes, and that he probably didn't even *own* a pair of work boots.

"Listen," Steven said to his old buddy. They were, after all, the two original founding members of the club, and had a special relationship.

"No, *you* listen, needle nose," Jerome said.

"Jerome," I bellowed, remembering I was in

charge. "Understand, if we go through with the court-martial, he's going to insist on calling in his own witnesses."

"Let him call—"

"Witnesses . . ." I continued, "which would include any and all individuals—be they He-Men, or girls, or Nessy—who might have witnessed the event—bringing them right in *here*, into the one reliable sanctuary. . . . Think about it, Jerome. Who knows when Vanessa'll get an uncontrollable attack of the kissies?"

Jerome's face, which was normally a shocking level of white, drained further into a sort of thin greenish film that barely concealed the veins and muscles of his face.

"Cut a deal," he croaked.

I opened the car door and hopped eagerly back inside. "All right," I bluffed. "You're a lucky guy, Wolf. The tribunal is in a very generous mood today, so we have agreed—out of respect and fondness for the history we've all shared here in the He-Man Women Haters Club—to forgo the formal, unpleasant process of a trial and allow you to leave quietly with a handshake and a dishonorable discharge."

At least Wolf had the courtesy to cover his

mouth with his hand during the early stages of his long laugh at me.

"You're such a kidder, Ling."

He knew very well that I am no such thing.

"Why would I want a dishonorable discharge from the club I love so dearly? First off, nobody really wants a dishonorable anything—that's not cool. Second, I didn't do anything wrong. Third, I'm going to win if we have a trial. And fourth, this'll be fun. The experience will bring us together, don't you think, because really, we've kind of drifted apart lately."

Clearly, Wolfgang had thought this through and had his heart set on a trial. If he wanted it, then for sure we did not. He was as frightening now—through that happy sinister grin—as he had ever been. A lesser man than myself would have admitted defeat right about now and begged him to let us out of this.

Boy, did I wish I were a lesser man.

"You know," I said sternly, "we could just kick you out without a trial."

"No you couldn't."

"What's to stop us?"

"I won't go," he said calmly.

"You won't— What do you mean you won't go?

That's the way things work, Wolfgang. Everybody in the world understands that if you get kicked out of someplace, you go."

"Not me, I don't."

"Then we'll throw you out. We can be pretty He-Man when we want to be, you know."

Again his hand politely covered his mouth. "I will ignore the obvious insanity of what you just said, and point out that if your club is caught throwing a defenseless handicapped boy out onto the street . . . well, you'll never hate women in this town again."

Wolf was by now so surely in charge of things, and so plainly aware of it, he turned away from me and pretended to be driving down the highway. "Can I drop you off anywhere?" he said cheerily.

"You are about as defenseless as a pit bull—"

"Thank you."

"On steroids—"

"Oh you're too kind."

"With a gun."

"Stop, you're embarrassing me. Anyway, I've got to fly, so let's make a date. Saturday suits me."

"All right, Wolf, you're on. But the jury is going to be He-Men only. That is not negotiable. Only official He-Man members can decide your fate."

"Hmmm," he said. I had him there. He was mean, but not unreasonable, and knew that we had to decide this among ourselves.

"Okay, I accept the He-Man jury, but on one condition."

God, get me out of this car before I promise him my first child.

"I want a judge to preside over the proceedings. A neutral party to make sure you guys don't railroad me."

"I'm going to be judge," I said.

"Ling, you expect to be prosecutor and jury member and witness and judge? Aren't we getting a little *Alice in Wonderland* here?"

"Fine," I sighed. "Who do you propose?"

"Your mom."

Whoa! There it was. The great tactical error. I knew he'd eventually make a fatal mistake, and there it was.

"*My* mom?" I asked coolly.

"Yes. She seems to be a fair and reasonable person, and I figured she would be acceptable to both parties. Is she acceptable to you, Ling?"

I tried to contain my glee.

"Um, I suppose we could accept this condition."

"Wonderful." He extended his hand. I took it and we shook.

"See you on Saturday," I said with professional dignity.

"Done," he said as he slid himself out his car door and into his waiting chariot. "Now, I'm off for my date with your sister. Wish me luck."

My whole body shivered. With either fear or disgust. I couldn't tell the difference anymore.

As soon as Wolf was gone, all the He-Men piled into the car wanting to know, "What happened, what happened? How'd it go?"

I folded my arms across my chest. "I toyed with him."

11
The Trial

It was like a parade of all the villains from all our previous episodes, filing into the garage behind smiling Wolfgang.

Rock was pushing him in the wheelchair.

Behind them, Nessy marched humorlessly, like the POWs part of the Memorial Day Parade.

Behind them Monica, leading her battalion of sly, never-turn-your-back-on-them Girl Scouts.

If Steven had a recurring nightmare that haunted his sleep, I'm sure it looked exactly like this.

On the bright side, Cecil had constructed a very nice courtroom for us. Using the pallets that were our stage platforms when we were rock stars, he had made a raised jury box for Steven, Jerome, and himself. My mother sat at the very back wall of the garage, in a maroon velour bucket seat that we had removed for the occasion from a Mustang

Lars had been restoring. The Lincoln itself was to serve as the jury deliberation room.

Wolfgang's rogue's gallery of supporters had to sit on the cold floor on cardboard squares laid over oil stains.

The witness stand, next to my mother, was a gray metal folding chair.

"I call my first witness, He-Man Jerome," I boomed. I figured I would hit him right off with the most enthusiastic of his accusers.

From across the room, Jerome just shook his head at me.

"Excuse me?" I said.

He shook his head some more. Remained frozen in the jury box like a taxidermist's hamster.

"Excuse me, your honor," I said to Mom. I scurried to Jerome. "What are you doing?" I whispered, whacking myself on the leg with my riding crop.

He stared straight ahead. "Maybe later. Start with somebody else."

"Grrrr," I growled at him. Regrouping, I said, "The prosecution calls He-Man Cecil."

Nervously, but with great strength and dignity, Cecil took the stand.

"State your name for the court, please," I said.

"I never been so a-scared in my whole life," he answered.

There were titters aplenty from the gallery.

"Cecil," I said, calmly, slowly. "That is not what I asked y—"

"I never been so a-scared in my whole—"

"Your witness," I said to Wolfgang, knowing when I was licked. Cecil's normally vacant eyes were practically emitting their own light at this point.

"Mr. Cecil," Wolfgang said warmly. "On the day of the alleged dance party, what exactly did you believe you were going to the Ling household to do?"

Cecil finally broke eye contact with space. He looked at Wolf. He looked newly startled.

"I never been so a-scared in—"

"Yes, we have established that. What were you going there to do?"

"I object," I called, jumping out of the jury box and waving the riding crop like a flag.

"Sit down, you, and wait your turn," the judge said.

"Maaaa?" I whined.

"Cecil, answer the question," she said.

"Mrffdedebrrrrr," he mumbled.

"A little louder, please?" Wolf asked.

"I thought we was gonna get tough with that little girl Nessy."

Everyone in the room gasped. The judge gasped. The prosecutor gasped.

"Well," Cecil pleaded, "it sounds worse now that I say it out loud . . . but at the time it seemed like good clean—"

Wolf cut in. "How would you expect to get tough with this girl when she had in fact on a previous occasion defeated three of you He-Men at once?"

"Well," Cecil answered sheepishly, "I *thought* we had you on our side this time. But I sure was mistaken."

"Get off the stand, you," the judge snapped. Cecil bolted out of there like a horse that was slapped on the rear with a riding crop . . . now *there's* an idea.

Score: Forces of Evil—1, Forces of Good—0.

"The prosecution calls He-Man Jerome to the stand."

Jerome shook his head no again.

"Oh this is unbelievable," I said. I turned to my mother. "My whole case is built around him. Make him testify."

"I can't play favorites with you now, Ling."

"But I *am* your favorite," I said desperately.

"I object," Wolf said. I suppose he had a point.

"No," Rock called from the audience. "He's right. He *is* her favorite, the little puke."

Mom slapped her hands together loudly. We couldn't find her a gavel. "I will have you removed from the court," she said to my sister. "But Jerome, you get up here now. You do have to testify, so please get on with it."

Now we were getting somewhere. "Jerome, will you please tell the court, in your own words, what happened to you on the day in question?"

Jerome, shaking like a madman and staring out into the gallery, hesitated before speaking. "Well," he finally said. "It was pretty dark down there . . . it was hard to even know who was . . ."

Oh no. They had gotten to him. This was one of those legal-thriller nightmares come true. I whipped around to see where Jerome was staring, and there was Nessy. She was making kissy faces at him.

"Jerome, I want you to know," I said, "that you have nothing to be afraid of here. You should feel completely free to tell the truth without worrying about any retaliation."

"Oh right," Jerome said, the old vigor returning. "So who's gonna protect me? You? You had your chance. Go ahead, lift up your shirt and show everybody the poke marks in your belly."

The judge stepped in. "Ling? Don't you dare lift your shirt here in front of all these people."

"Face the facts," Jerome went on. "The only He-Man tough enough to protect me is that rat over there." He pointed at the defendant, who smiled shyly. "And *you* want me to testify against him." He leaned forward as he said it, and jabbed me in the belly with his finger.

It was actually rather touching, the way Wolfgang took over the cross examination. He quietly wheeled up behind me and rubbed my back, like a manager removing a pitcher from the game when he tells him, "Sorry kid, it just ain't your day."

"Jerome," he started, his voice sickly sweet. "You don't really want me thrown out of the club now, do you?"

"Yes I do," Jerome snapped. "You're scary and you're tricky and you do whatever you feel like and *I* don't think you even hate women at all, so what do you think of that?"

It had gotten impossible to tell, anymore,

whether Jerome was helping the case or hurting it. Or even which side he wanted to be on.

"Oh" was Wolf's startled reply.

"And everybody in the club is afraid of you anyway."

Wolf, pumped up with pride, turned to the jury box. Steven bared his teeth.

"You can go now," Wolfgang said.

As he passed by Wolfgang, Jerome snarled at him, "You *should* be a lawyer, ya rat."

It was time to put this away before Wolf could do any more damage.

"He-Man Steven," I announced, as if I was introducing royalty. As Steven rose and headed for the witness stand, the entire garage went deadly quiet.

Both sides were aware *this* would be an event.

"Remember," I said in his ear as I escorted him to the stand. "This is the moment you've been waiting for. We need to pull together here. I know you've been through a terrible ordeal, and we don't want to dredge it all up, but let's get the job done. I'll lead you through it."

He nodded, took the seat.

"Steven, as the founding father of the He-Man Women Haters Club—"

Hisses, low boooos came from the crowd at the mention of the sacred name.

"Can you tell us the principles your organization was built on?"

"We hate women," he answered robotically.

More booos, more hisses. Somebody threw a chewed piece of gum that bounced off Steven's forehead. The impartial judge leaned over and said, "If you were my son, I'd put you over my knee."

"No offense, your honor, but if I was him, I'd put myself over a cliff."

"Yes, yes," I cut in. "And when He-Man Wolf joined, was he aware what you were all about?"

"He was."

"And did it appear to you, in your original meetings with Wolfgang, that he did, in fact, hate women?"

"It seemed to me that Wolfgang hated all living things, which I assumed would include women things."

"Fair enough. Now Steven, I realize you've been through a horrifying experience, but could you please try to recall the afternoon of the dance party—"

"Objection," called the defendant. "*Alleged* dance party."

"What?" Steven leaned forward in his seat and grabbed me by the shirt. "I thought we were going to avoid this."

"If you want to get him out, we have to have the smoking gun."

Steven sat back, took a deep breath.

"Um, he tricked us into thinking we were having a summit meeting to get Vanessa to stop harassing Jerome. Then when we got there, the lights went out, and Nessy got ahold of Jerome, and . . . girls everywhere . . . music . . . lights low . . . snacks . . . girls . . ."

"Steve-o, Steve-o," I said, putting a hand on his shoulder to calm him. "Easy there, buddy. Now, please, could you tell the court what happened when Monica dragged you into the paint closet and kept you trapped for seven whole minutes?"

There was a very long pause as Steven composed himself. He looked out over the crowd, which was also silent. Silent, that is, except for one very excited Girl Scout who could not help giggling throughout this whole portion of the trial.

"I don't know what you're talking about."

I looked at Steven, then back at the crowd, then back at Steven again. "Pardon me?"

"I said I don't know what you mean. I never went into any closet with any girl."

"Steven?"

"I didn't and I never would, everybody knows that. In fact, I don't even know anybody named Monica. Sorry, never met her."

Now we had a near riot. Representatives of both sides wanted a piece of Steven. Monica jumped up and screamed—backed by her Girl Scout friends, The Monicats. "You filthy pig. You cowardly little hairless dog—"

Oh boy. Right for the jugular, eh, Monica?

"Hey," Steven screamed back. "I got hairs. I got loads of hair, all over the place, I got hairs." As he said it, he made a broad sweeping gesture with his arm, as if he had hairs all over the garage.

"Sit down, all of you," the judge hollered.

I took advantage of the moment to lean close to Steven and offer him a little professional advice. "See, Steven, the key to effective lying is to say something that cannot be disproven by every person in the room, including the judge."

He sat back, crossed his arms defiantly. "Ya, well, that's my story. I never met her before. And even if I had, nothing would have happened in that paint room. Nothing."

"Sheesh," I said, hobbling away once more from the witness stand.

Wolfgang was practically salivating.

"Hi," he said.

Steven refused to answer.

"Fine. Steven, will you please tell the court what desperate and pathetic nickname you have given to yourself?"

"I'm gonna kick your—"

"I'm sorry, could you speak up so everybody can hear you?"

"Johnny Chesthair," Steven said proudly. "And I didn't give the name to myself. It just sort of—"

"Isn't that sad?" Wolf cut in. "Okay. Johnny, when the He-Men went on television one time, there was a moment toward the end of the program when the pressure was really on—"

"Nothing happened," Steven snapped.

"May I remind you that we have the event on a very popular and widely circulated video?"

"I threw up, all right? So what's your point, bat ears?"

"I would like to state, for the record, that Steven hurt my feelings with that reference to the pointiness of my ears."

"Oh please," Steven sighed. "*What* feelings?"

"You may step down and stop soiling my witness stand, rotten boy," Mom said.

That would be a problem, the judge hating your star witness.

"You got any more witnesses?" Wolf asked me.

I barely had the strength to shake my head no.

"Good. I'll be brief. The defense calls Monica."

That's right, Wolfie, as long as we're down, just keep kicking away there, boy. All you had to do was watch her stroll to the stand, and you could feel the red menace of her. Bright shiny pigtails hanging perfect, motionless, the tips like epaulets on the shoulders of her Girl Scout uniform. Her patent-leather shoes more highly polished than my own. She smiled at everyone, waved at her friends when she took the stand, then shared a stick of Trident with the judge.

"Now Monica, would you like to add anything to what Steven said about that afternoon in the paint room?"

"He kisses like a fish."

It was good that Wolf dismissed her at that point, since the laughter and squealing made it impossible to hear any more anyway. Steven tipped all the way over backward in his chair, crashing to the floor. Then he didn't bother to get back up.

Wolf was on a roll.

"I call . . . He-Man Ling-Ling to the stand."

"What? No I'm very busy . . . being a prosecutor . . . being on the jury . . . sorry."

"Get up here," he said.

Slowly, I did. Very slowly.

I sat there in the witness stand, waiting, waiting, trying to hold it together. Wolf wheeled right up to me and just smiled. He looked friendly enough, but . . . god was I afraid of him. What was he going to do to me? What was to be *my* humiliation? I was the one, the mastermind, the person responsible for this whole situation. What was he going to do? Why didn't he get it over with, for god's sake? Have some mercy. . . .

I could feel the tears rolling like golf balls down my face.

He spoke solemnly. "Let the record show that the prosecutor is crying tears of *shame* for what he has done to me."

He didn't break stride, calling himself to the witness stand before I'd even vacated it. He rolled up, parked his chair right in front of me, and addressed the crowd.

"So you see, everybody, all I've ever wanted to do is improve their chances of survival. I just want to help my brother He-Men to achieve their real goal—

they want to become men. And as we can plainly see, you couldn't take the whole gang of them together, put them in a blender, and come out with one decent man. They are so desperately in need of help, extraordinary measures were in order."

"Ain't that the truth," the judge murmured, knowing full well her son could hear her clearly from the witness stand.

"I mean," Wolf went on, "the president, Ling, has been running around lately looking like a kids' breakfast cereal commercial. I tried to tell them, the girls like me because I'm dangerous and exciting. Superheroes are for goofs; *villains* is where it's at. Everybody knows that. But do they listen? No.

"So I just want to say, if I am guilty, then I guess I'm just guilty of trying too hard. I tried the only way I know to make men out of these boys—I tried to make them more like me.

"Ladies and gentlemen, I'm sure you can sympathize. You've all seen what I had to work with."

Well, at the very least, Wolfgang accomplished one thing—he made hamburger out of the club that was about to bounce him. But that didn't matter. No matter how stupid we looked, we were back in charge. The vote belonged to the He-Men.

12

Justice, the Long Way Around

We huddled inside the jury deliberation-mobile.

"This shouldn't take too long," I said. "I vote he's out."

Steven jumped in. "He's out. Let's hurry and get him and his gang out the door before the odor of girl wipes out all the motor oil and paint and other good smells."

Then came the shocker.

"I vote he stays," said Jerome.

"What?" Steven said. "You little mental case! What do you want to do that for, after all he did to you?"

"Because he's right," Jerome said. "Like it or not, villains is where it's at. It would be boring without him."

"And Nessy'd eat you for breakfast?" I suggested.

"That too," he added unapologetically.

"Fine," I said. "We'll call yours a protest vote. It's just symbolic anyway, because it'll be three to one—"

Cecil started shaking his head.

"Now don't *you* start," Steven said.

"I just don't see why we should kick him out if all he was tryin' to do was help us. I was confused there until he pointed it out, but now I know what he was doin' . . . and we oughta be ashamed we didn't even appreciate it. He had me almost in tears myself when—"

"*I'll* have you in tears," Steven said, lunging over the seat at Cecil.

I stuck myself between them. "All right, that's enough now. This is just great—now what are we going to do?"

On cue, the back door of the Lincoln opened, and Wolf threw himself in, right out of his wheelchair. "Come on, push over now, push over."

With the five of us assembled in such tight quarters, it was a little tense.

"You have to get out," I said calmly. "This is where the jury is supposed to deliberate in secret."

"I know, that's why I'm here. I'm voting."

"What?" we all asked him at once.

95

"Sure, the jury is made up of all the He-Men, just as we agreed. No matter what the outcome of the trial, I am still, as of this moment, a He-Man, am I not?"

"Crap," Steven said, already conceding defeat.

"I'm getting a ruling from the judge," I said, popping the door open.

Wolf put a hand on my back. "Are you starting to *enjoy* public humiliation?"

I sat back down.

"Don't gloat," I said. "All right, everybody, let's make it quick. Out!" I said.

"Out," said Steven.

"In," said Jerome.

"Good boy," said Wolf, winking at him.

"In," said Cecil.

Taking his time, cracking his knuckles, breathing deep the air of victory, Wolf finally voiced his vote.

"Out!" he said with a big rotten smile.

I could not believe my ears. But I guess I should not be surprised by anything my ears tell me at this point.

"You're bluffing," Steven said.

"No way. If I'm caught with this weenie club one more second, I'm afraid my reputation might never recover from it. It's been fun, boys."

On that word, he slipped back out of the car and into his chair. The four remaining He-Men crawled up tight to the rear window and stared, slack jawed, as he made his way out the far door of the garage. He was surrounded by his gang of girls—Vanessa riding in the chair with him, Rock rubbing his back, Monica unwrapping a stick of gum for him. Like *he* was the victim.

Steven broke the silence, speaking with what sounded a little like admiration as the door closed on The Trial of Wolfgang.

"Now *that* was a butt whipping."

Here's a brief look at
THE WOLF GANG,
the next book in the
He-Man Women Haters Club series.
Don't miss it!

Gangin' Up

We were at the club, hanging out, doing nothing much but sitting in, on, or under my beautiful black Lincoln. No heavy lifting, no major brain-wave motion disrupting things. Just the way a guy likes it.

Until the mail came. Now understand that in the six months or so the He-Man Women Haters Club had been in existence, we had previously received three pieces of mail.

So when a piece of mail came to Lars's garage addressed to the HMWHC, we noticed. And when the return address read from THE WOLF GANG, we ducked.

I tore the letter open with my teeth, to the gape-mouthed amazement of my troops.

"What a stupid name anyway," I said before reading. "The Wolf Gang. Pathetic. You'd think he could at least come up with a tougher-sounding . . ."

"Like He-Man," Jerome prodded, "or Johnny Chesthair."

"Don't get fresh," I said.

I read the letter out loud (after a quick silent run-through to make sure there were no trick three- or four-syllable words lurking in there):

Dear Comrades,

Even though you guys tried to railroad me and court-martial me and hang me by the neck until dead, I hold no hard feelings. As a matter of fact I've been thinking, as I kick back in the comfort of my impressive new club-house, what a shame it is that we can't all be together again. We sure had some rockin' times back there in the early days of the club, before you got all screwed up. I'd like to try and make things better, because I am a big person, and extend to your club an invitation to come visit me and mine at my new club, The Wolf Gang. Don't you love the name?

Anyway, I have to go now, very busy Wolf-banging around, you see. But please come by next Saturday, take the tour, have a cold Yoo-Hoo, and renew old times.

> *Sincere as always,*
> *Prince Wolfgang I*
> *Absolute Ruler*
> *Defender of the Faith*
> *Chief Executive Officer*
> *Party Guy*
> *Sacred Order of the*
> *Gang of Wolf*

P.S. If Steven is too afraid to come, I understand.

Oh, boy, oh boy, can Wolfgang chew a raw nerve like a dog on a ham bone, or what? Afraid? Me? Of *him*? That'll be the day. That . . . will . . . be . . . the . . . day. I don't fear him, I just hate him. There's a great big difference. But he wouldn't understand that.

"Can you believe this cheese ball?" I said to my troops. "Trying to say that I, Johnny Chesthair, am afraid of a rat like him. . . . Get a load of this guy, will ya? He'll say anything to get attention."

I laughed my patented brave laugh. Laughed it long, laughed it hard.

Laughed it alone.

"What?" I said when I realized my boys were a little skeptical. "What? You don't *buy* it, do you?"

"Well," Jerome answered gently, "Wolf always did have a way of getting to you."

"But it is all right, ain't it?" Cecil asked naively. "For a guy to be afraid once in a while? I mean, sometimes, bein' afraid just makes sense."

"No, it is not all right," I said. "We do not be afraid. It does not make sense. It is not allowed."

"Well," Cecil went on, "forgive me for bein' simple here, but seems to me that you break your own rule sometimes. 'Cause the way you act all panicky and deranged whenever that girl Monica—"

"That's *different*!" I blurted. "That's not fear, that's confusion. Because she is a deceptive and unpredictable opponent who plays by no known set of rules, and who will stoop as low as humanly possible to bring down her enemy. That is confusion, not fear. Confusion. Not fear. Confusion . . ."

Cecil was satisfied, even impressed with my response. Not so the others. Ling shook his head dubiously. Jerome openly laughed at me.

"What's your problem?" I asked.

"Her *enemy*? You, are her enemy?" Jerome asked.

"Steven, if what Monica does to you is how she treats her enemies, what does she do when she *likes* somebody? Fetch their slippers with her teeth? Throw money at them? Lay her coat over mud puddles for them to walk over?"

You cannot reason with Jerome when he gets like this. You have to just move on. "Obviously," I said calmly, "you have fallen for her ploy."

"Colonel?" Ling called with his hand raised.

Now here was a He-Man I could talk to. I acknowledged him with a regal nod.

"I hate to disagree with you, but it just seems, from the way your hand is shaking with that letter in it, and the way your eyes keep rolling all the way back in your head every time anyone mentions Wolfgang . . ."

God, I hated the sound of that name.

". . . Ya, just like you're doing right now. Well, sir, this would seem to indicate that it may be true, that you harbor a little fear of Wolf."

"That is not fear!" I insisted once more. "That is anger. Anger is good. And it is rage. Rage is good. Anger and rage are good. They make a guy strong. They are good. They are good, not fear. Fear bad. Anger, rage good."

Apparently, that didn't come out the way I'd

intended it. The three of them stared back at me with even more concern than before I started explaining.

"Fine," I snapped. "We'll go to the stupid Wolf stupid Gang stupid Club and take the stupid tour and drink a stupid Yoo–stupid Hoo and then you'll see that stupid Wolf and his stupid Gang don't bother me at all. Is that what you want? You want to put Johnny to the test?'

They shrugged and nodded at the same time, all three of them. A forceful, decisive outfit, my men.

"Okay," I said. "Just you remember, the last time we let what's-his-gang lead us blindly into a pow-wow, we were ambushed into . . ."

I paused, forced my voice down into the very bottom of its manly range.

". . . a *dance party*," I rumbled.

A chill went through the room.